Sammy Wakes His Dad

By Chip Emmons
Illustrated by Shirley Venit Anger

Star Bright Books
New York

Library of Congress Cataloging-in-Publication Data

Emmons, Chip.
Sammy wakes his dad / by Chip Emmons ; illustrated by Shirley Venit Anger.
p. cm.
Summary: Sammy's father, who is in a wheelchair, is reluctant to join Sammy in going fishing, until his son's love finally moves him to action.
ISBN 1-887734-87-2
[1. Fathers and sons--Fiction. 2. Wheelchairs--Fiction. 3. Physically handicapped--Fiction. 4. Fishing--Fiction.] I. Anger, Shirley Venit, ill. II. Title.
PZ7.E6962 Sam 2002
[E]--dc21

2001004101

Published by Star Bright Books, Inc.

Printed in China 9 8 7 6 5 4 3 2 1

Sammy loved fishing. His dad had taught him how. Early every morning he got out of bed and put on in his digging pants and favorite fishing shirt.

Then he quietly tiptoed down the stairs,
opened the creaky back door and put on his boots.

He made his way to the old red garden shed. There he grabbed his shovel, fishing rod, tackle box, and the rusty worm pail.

Sammy knew the best spots to find worms. His father had taught him that, too.

He pushed the shovel into the moist ground and lifted up a clump of earth. “Wake up, worms,” he said. “Time to go fishing.” The worms tried to wriggle back into the crumbling soil, but Sammy was too quick for them.

Soon the bottom of the pail was covered with wriggling worms. “Done,” said Sammy as he picked up his gear and headed for the dock.

Carefully, Sammy slipped a worm onto a hook. "Where are you, big fellahs?" he called to the fish as he cast his line. "Come and bite."

But he didn't really care whether he caught a fish or not. Most of the time they were too small anyway, and had to be thrown back into the lake.

Sammy loved being outside, seeing the heron fishing at the edge of the lake, the bright dragonflies flashing past in the sunlight, and the water bugs skipping about on the surface of the water. All this he had shared with his dad, and Sammy missed having him at his side.

Sammy loved listening to the loons and hearing the busy twittering of the birds in the oak and birch trees.

But when his mom called him for breakfast, he reeled in his line and headed back home.

On the way home, he returned the remaining worms to the moist spot he had taken them from.

Then he put away his fishing gear and walked toward the house. Sammy could see his dad sitting, as he always did, in the bay window, watching him.

At breakfast Sammy talked about the heron, who was always there, as well as all the other birds and the insects he had seen. His dad smiled wistfully as he listened.

He also told his dad about the fish, and to cheer him up, Sammy said, "You should have seen it, Dad, the one that got away. It was THIS BIG," and he stretched out his arms as far as they would go. It was the same every day.

But one morning it was different. Instead of saying, "You should have seen it, Dad . . ." Sammy said, "Dad, will you come fishing tomorrow? I miss you, and I don't like fishing on my own. I want you to come with me."

His father was quiet for a moment and then said, "You know I love fishing, but it's hard for me to get around since the accident."

"I know," said Sammy. "But you've got wheels! You can still get around and do all sorts of things." His father's eyes filled with tears, but all he said was, "It's time for school."

That day, while Sammy was at school, his father thought about Sammy's words. "Sammy's right," he said to himself. "I've got wheels, and I'll use them!" And guiding his wheelchair, he made his way to the old shed and went inside. "Things will change," he said as he reached for the rusty old worm pail.

For hours he sanded the pail. When all the rust was gone he opened some tins of model paint and painted a picture of a boy and his father fishing together. The boy was reeling in a "big one" from the water.

When Sammy got home from school he helped his father make dinner.

When his mom came home, they enjoyed the meal together. Everything was the same.

Sammy and his mother talked about their day, and although his father was as quiet as usual, he seemed happier. Every now and then he smiled to himself. Sammy wondered what was up.

The next morning Sammy woke with the sun as usual. He dressed quickly and headed out to the red shed. He reached for the shovel but it was gone. In its place was the worm pail. Sammy grabbed the pail and and rushed out of the shed.

He ran toward the figure he saw sitting where the best worms were. "Dad!" yelled Sammy. "The pail is beautiful! Are you going fishing with me?"

"Not unless you get some worms first!" his father replied.

For about an hour they cast and reeled and cast and reeled. They watched the heron fishing and listened to the loons. They saw ripples from surfacing fish while the morning light danced on the water. They caught no fish and did not care. For the two fishermen, it was a magical time, a new beginning.